A *Jesus in My Little Pocket* Book

JESUS IN MY POCKET 4 little

Children, come and listen to me.
I will teach you to worship the Lord.
Psalm 34:11

Thomas Nelson Publishers
Nashville

Jesus, Jesus Everywhere
A *Jesus in My Little Pocket* Book

Jesus in My Pocket Ministries
PMB #327
6632 Telegraph Road
Bloomfield, MI 48301

Printed in Mexico

1 2 3 4 5 6 . . . 04 03 02 01 00 99

I feel Jesus everywhere...

Where I least
expect Him
to be.
His blessings
they are all
around,
If I just look
and see.

The Word says...

My Father will give you anything you ask for in my name.

John 16:23

With Love

Jesus in My Little Pocket

Fold Here

FROM: ________________

TO: ________________

____

I see Jesus everywhere...

Where I least
expect Him
to be,
Like high
above the
clouds and
sun
Looking down
at me!

The Word says...

They will see the Son of Man coming on clouds in the sky.

Matthew 24:30

With L♥ve

Jesus in My Little Pocket

Fold Here

FROM: ______________

TO: ______________

____

I see Jesus everywhere...

Where I least
expect Him
to be,
Like in my
crunchy
apple,
Or a pie baked
just for me.

The Word says...

God fills the hungry with good things.

Luke 1:53

Jesus in My Little Pocket

With L♥V

Fold Here

FROM: ______________

TO: ______________

____

I see Jesus everywhere...

Where I least
  expect Him
  to be,
Like in my yard,
  and in my
  house,
And underneath
  my favorite
  tree.

The Word says...

He has put his angels in charge of you.
  They will watch over you.

Psalm 91:11

With L♥V

Jesus in My Little Pocket

Fold Here

FROM: ______________

TO: ______________

____

I see Jesus everywhere...

Where I least
expect Him
to be,
Like in my
mother's
flowers,
Among the
bumble bees.

The Word says...

Blossoms appear through all the land.
The time has come to sing.

Song of Solomon 2:12

With Love

Jesus in My Little Pocket

Fold Here

FROM: ____________

TO: ____________

____

I see Jesus everywhere...

Where I least
expect Him
to be,
Like on the
beach at sun-
set,
And in the
sparkling sea.

The Word says...

He spread out the earth on the seas.
His love continues forever.

Psalm 136:6

With Love

Jesus in My Little Pocket

Fold Here

FROM: ______________

TO: ______________

____

I see Jesus everywhere...

Where I least
expect Him
to be,
Like in the smil-
ing faces
Of my friends
and family.

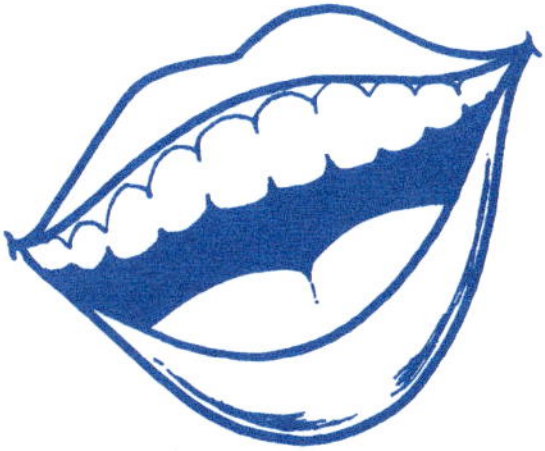

The Word says...

My true brother and sister and mother are those who do the things God wants.

Mark 3:35

Jesus in My Little Pocket

With Love

Fold Here

FROM: ____________

TO: ____________

____

I see Jesus everywhere...

Where I least
expect Him
to be,
Like in my
Grandma's
kisses,
And on my
Grandpa's
knee.

The Word says...

Grandchildren are the reward of old people.

Proverbs 17:6

With L♥V

Jesus in My Little Pocket

Fold Here

FROM: ______________

TO: ______________

____

I see Jesus everywhere...

Where I least
expect Him
to be,
Like in my toys,
my bike, my
dolls,
And my favorite
fuzzy teddy.

The Word says...

He gives us everything to enjoy.

I Timothy 6:17

With L♥V

Jesus in My Little Pocket

Fold Here

FROM: ____________

TO: ____________

____

I feel Jesus everywhere...

Where I least
expect Him
to be.
I feel Him when
I'm brave and
kind,
To those who'd
like to harm
me.

The Word says...

Being afraid of people can get you into
trouble.
But if you trust the Lord, you will be
safe.

Proverbs 29:25

With L♥V

Jesus in My Little Pocket

Fold Here

FROM: ____________

TO: ____________

____

I feel Jesus everywhere...

Where I least
expect Him
to be.
And if I acci-
dentally sin
I know that He
forgives me.

The Word says...

Jesus said, "Your sins are forgiven."

Luke 7:48

With Love

Jesus in My Little Pocket

Fold Here

FROM: ____________

TO: ____________

____

I feel Jesus everywhere...

Where I least
expect Him
to be.
He brings me
comfort,
hears my
prayers,
And lends a
hand to guide me.

The Word says...

This God is our God forever and ever.
He will guide us from now on.

Psalm 48:14

Jesus in My Little Pocket

With Love

Fold Here

FROM: ____________

TO: ____________

____

I feel Jesus everywhere...

Where I least
 expect Him
 to be.
Like when I'm
 feeling really
 sad,
I know that
 He's beside
 me.

The Word says...

The Lord is my strength and shield.
 I trust him, and he helps me.

Psalm 28:7

With Love

Jesus in My Little Pocket

Fold Here

FROM: ____________

TO: ____________

____

I feel Jesus everywhere...

Where I least
  expect Him
  to be.
I know when I
  forgive a hurt,
Jesus forgives
  me.

The Word says...

If you forgive others for the things they do wrong, then your Father in heaven will also forgive you for the things you do wrong.

Matthew 6:14

Jesus in My Little Pocket

With Love

Fold Here

FROM: ________________

TO: ________________

____

I see Jesus everywhere...

Where I least
expect Him
to be,
Like in my
Daddy's great
big hug
When he comes
home to me.

The Word says...

And the world will know that you loved these people the same as you loved me.

John 17:23

Jesus in My Little Pocket

With L♥V

Fold Here

FROM: ______________

TO: ______________

____

I see Jesus everywhere...

Where I least
expect Him
to be,
He's in the
farmyard, in
the meadow,
And in every
city.

The Word says...

You will be blessed in the city. You will be blessed in the country.

Deuteronomy 28:3

With L♥V

Jesus in My Little Pocket

Fold Here

FROM: ____________

TO: ____________

____

I see Jesus everywhere...

Where I least
expect Him
to be,
He's high up
inside heaven,
Watching over
me.

The Word says...

The One who comes from heaven is greater than all.

John 3:31

Jesus in My Little Pocket

With L♥V

Fold Here

FROM: ____________

TO: ____________

____

I see Jesus everywhere...

Where I least
expect Him
to be.
He's in the way
my playmate
laughs,
When we're act-
ing silly.

The Word says...

A friend loves you all the time.

Proverbs 17:17

With Love

Jesus in My Little Pocket

Fold Here

FROM: ________________

TO: ________________

____

I see Jesus everywhere...

Where I least
expect Him
to be.
He's in the rain-
drops as they
fall,
And as they
soak right
through me.

The Word says...

He blesses you with rain from above.
He blesses you with water from springs
below.

Genesis 49:25

Jesus in My Little Pocket

With Love

Fold Here

FROM: ________________

TO: ________________

____

I see Jesus everywhere...

Where I least
expect Him
to be.
He's there
inside my
Mom and
Dad,
And everyone
who loves me.

The Word says...

If we love each other, God lives in us. If we love each other, God's love has reached its goal.

I John 4:12

With Love

Jesus in My Little Pocket

Fold Here

FROM: ______________

TO: ______________

____

I feel Jesus everywhere...

Where I least
expect Him
to be.
I know He's
always by my
side,
So I don't need
to worry.

The Word says...

Don't let your hearts be troubled. Don't be afraid.

John 14:27

With L♥V

Jesus in My Little Pocket

Fold Here

- -

FROM: ________________

TO: ________________

____

I feel Jesus everywhere...

Where I least
expect Him
to be.
When I bow my
head and say
my prayers,
I know He
always hears
me.

The Word says...

I love the Lord because he listens
to my prayers for help.

Psalm 116:1

With Love

Jesus in My Little Pocket

Fold Here

FROM: ____________

TO: ____________

____

I feel Jesus everywhere...

Where I least
expect Him
to be.
He's in the
pages of my
Bible,
In my church
on Sunday.

The Word says...

Your word is a lamp for my feet
and a light for my way.

Psalm 119:105

With Love

Jesus in My Little Pocket

Fold Here

FROM: ____________________

TO: ____________________

____

I feel Jesus everywhere...

Where I least
expect Him
to be.
He is peace, and
He is love,
And He lives
right inside
me.

The Word says...

I leave you peace. My peace I give you.

John 14:27

With Love

Jesus in My Little Pocket

Fold Here

FROM: ______________

TO: ______________

____

I feel Jesus everywhere...

Where I least
expect Him
to be.
He holds my
hand, He
makes me
strong,
He's always
there to guide me.

The Word says...

The Lord your God will go with you. He will not leave you or forget you.

Deuteronomy 31:6

With Love

Jesus in My Little Pocket

Fold Here

FROM: ____________________

TO: ____________________

____

I feel Jesus everywhere...

Where I least
 expect Him
 to be.
I know He
 speaks into
 my heart,
He tells me that
 He loves me.

The Word says...

We know the love that God has for us, and we trust that love.

I John 4:16

Jesus in My Little Pocket

With L♥V

Fold Here

FROM: ______________

TO: ______________

____

I feel Jesus everywhere...

Where I least
expect Him
to be.
He sits beside
me day and
night,
He keeps me
company.

The Word says...

The Lord's eyes see everything that happens.

Proverbs 15:3

With Love

Jesus in My Little Pocket

Fold Here

FROM: ____________________

TO: ____________________

____

I feel Jesus everywhere...

Where I least
expect Him
to be.
I snuggle down
to dream at
night,
He watches
over me.

The Word says...

I go to bed and sleep in peace.
Lord, only you keep me safe.

Psalm 4:8

To accept Jesus Christ as your personal Lord and Savior, pray out loud:

Father God, because I believe that Jesus was Your Son, died on the Cross and was raised from the dead for me and my sins, I am saved!